W9-APR-670

STECK-VAUGHN

PAIR-IT BOOKS™

Bear Facts

Written by Gare Thompson

STECK-VAUGHN®
C O M P A N Y
ELEMENTARY • SECONDARY • ADULT • LIBRARY

Black bears are big bears.

Black bears are good climbers.

Polar bears are bigger than black bears.

Polar bears are good swimmers.

Brown bears are bigger than polar bears.

Brown bears are good fishers.

Mother bears are bigger than bear cubs.